Chibi Samurai
Wants a Pet

An Adventure with
Little Kunoichi the Ninja Girl

Written and Illustrated
by SANAE ISHIDA

little bigfoot
an imprint of sasquatch books
seattle, wa

Little Kunoichi, a ninja-girl-in-training, has a pet.

But not just any pet . . .

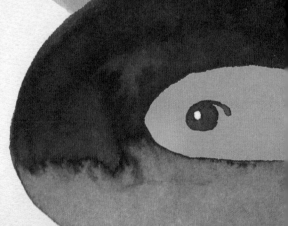

a stupendously, spectacularly
SUPER-DUPER NINJA BUNNY!

Little Kunoichi and Ninja Bunny
share and do everything together . . .

including playing with their best friend, Chibi Samurai.

OW!

THANKS, BUNNY,
I DON'T THINK I
NEED A GURNEY

I wish I had my very own pet,
thinks Chibi. *Look how they
comfort and care for each
other and have oodles of fun.
A pet is a friend and a snuggly
companion. I want that.*

He takes out his trusty map . . .

chooses a helmet from his *bushi* gear
(*bushi* is another way to say samurai),

IT MIGHT GET
DANGEROUS
OUT THERE

and goes off on his quest!

He starts at the tippy top of the island and greets a kindly monk.

Lo and behold, Chibi finds a
dazzling animal, and he can't
wait to introduce his new pet.

FANTASTIC!

"So fierce! So strong!
Meet Showstopper the
giant salamander!"

"Too strong!"

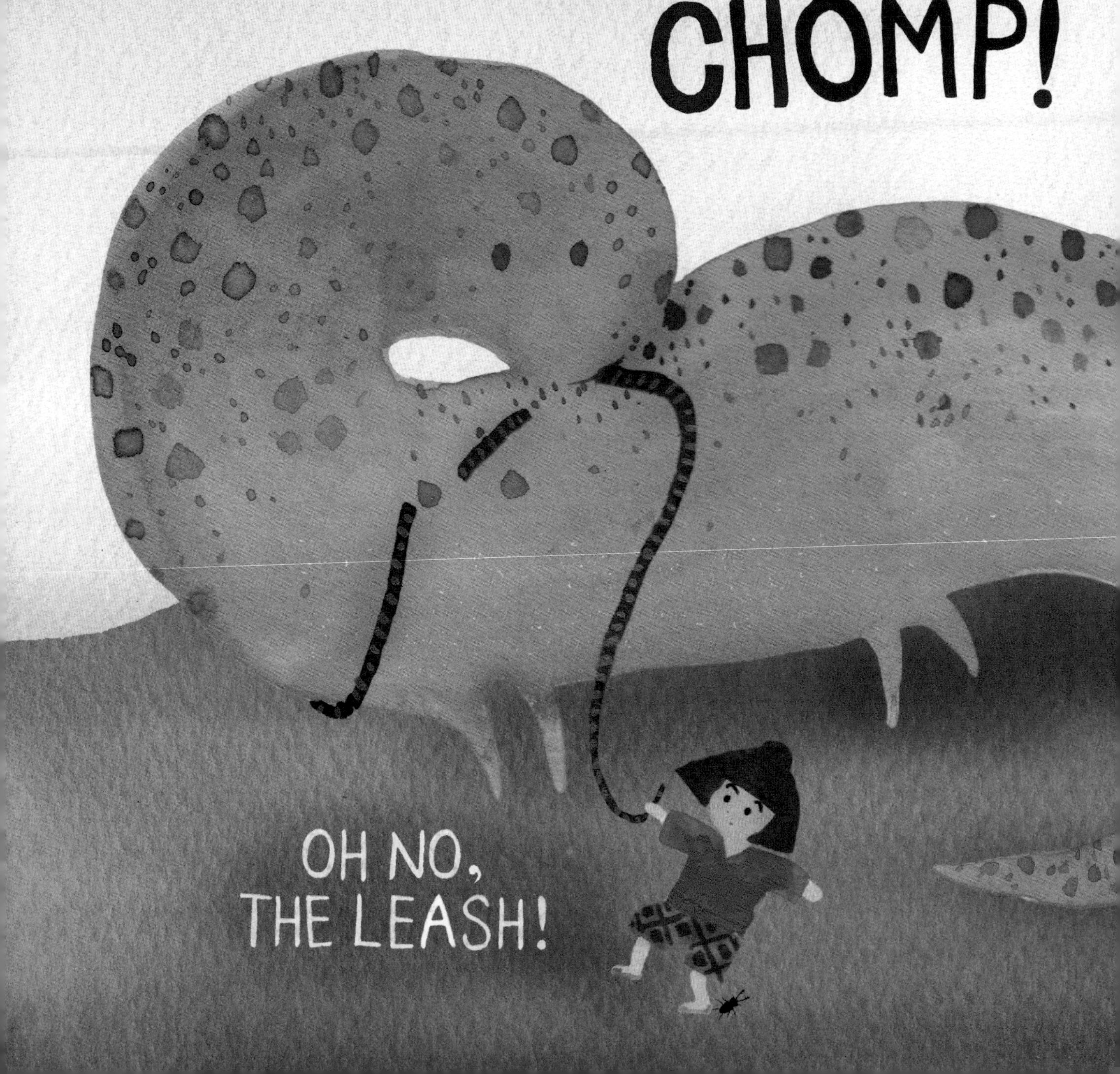

Exploring the forested lands filled with flora and fauna, Chibi spots a splendid critter. Could *this* be the pet of his dreams?

YOWZA!

"This is Capricious, a *tanuki*,"
says Chibi Samurai.
"So magical! So clever!
It can turn into anything!"

POOF!

TANUKI   COPYCAT BUNNY

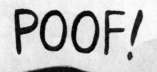

VROOM
C-YA
ONWARD AND UPWARD, MY FRIEND,
ONWARD AND UPWARD
SAYONARA

In the murk and mystery
of the marshy swamp,
Chibi makes a discovery.

HOORAY!

"I call it, uh . . . Au Contraire," says Chibi Samurai. "It's a water-dwelling *kappa*. So rare! So exotic!"

It's also stinky and slimy and *not* a fan of humans.

Chibi keeps searching . . .

and searching.

OPERATION STUPENDOUSLY, SPECTACULARLY SUPER PET

The quest is
not going well.

"You are so so *so* lucky to have such a great pet," Chibi tells Little Kunoichi.

"Maybe we can share bunny?"

"Thanks, but that's OK. I'll keep looking. There's a pet out there for me. I just know it!"

don't hate me because I'm enviable

FRANKLY, BUNNY IS A BIT MUCH SOMETIMES

Disappointed, Chibi wanders
around his neighborhood.

HELMET
SHOPPE

MAYBE
I NEED
ANOTHER
HELMET

SALE

And then he notices something . . .

small and shiny perched
on his shoulder:

A STAG
BEETLE

WINGS!

ÜBER
STRENGTH!

FUN!

It isn't what he expected,
or how he imagined he'd find it.

It's not big and showy.
Or full of magic tricks.
Or exceptional in every way.

But the tiny yet mighty
and loyal stag beetle
is just the right pet for him.

HELLO

CHIRP!

And guess what?
It was with Chibi the whole time!
(Did you see it?)

Often overlooked
All the treasures that we seek
Are here, part of us

stupendously, spectacularly
SUPER-DUPER

GO GO GO GO STAGOSAURUS!

Stag beetles are called *kuwagata* in Japanese, and the name refers to a samurai helmet style. They are popular pets in Japan. They live an average of three to five years and hibernate in the winter. Though beetles can be caught in the wild, they are often bought from pet stores. Some beetles can cost one thousand dollars!

Hanetsuki is a game similar to badminton played with wooden paddles and a shuttlecock. There is no net.

Macaque monkeys like to lounge in hot springs.

Many countries have a bigfoot or sasquatch legend, including Japan!

Bunny plays an instrument called shamisen, which is a lute.

Did you know?

The Japanese word for giant salamander, *ōsanshōuo*, means "giant pepper fish."

Serows are a combination of a mountain goat and antelope found in the forests and mountains of Japan.

The baby dragons are sitting on traditional Japanese rice barrels.

Fukuwarai is a Japanese version of pin the tail on the donkey. It's usually a woman's face instead of a donkey.

Tanukis are raccoon dogs, and there are many folk stories in Japan about how they are able to transform into any shape.

Kappa are mythical Japanese water creatures that are considered mischievous and sly.

The cloth-weaving crane is in reference to a famous Japanese folktale.

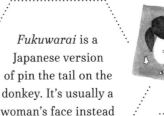

For my small yet mighty
furoku lovelies

Manufactured in China by C&C Offset Printing Co. Ltd.
Shenzhen, Guangdong Province, in April 2017

Published by Little Bigfoot, an imprint of Sasquatch Books

21 20 19 18 17   9 8 7 6 5 4 3 2 1

Editors: Tegan Tigani, Christy Cox
Production editor: Emma Reh
Design: Bryce de Flamand

Library of Congress Cataloging-in-Publication Data is available.

ISBN: 978-1-63217-117-7

Sasquatch Books
1904 Third Avenue, Suite 710
Seattle, WA 98101
(206) 467-4300
www.sasquatchbooks.com
custserv@sasquatchbooks.com